The
White Hare
and the Crocodile

by Sue Graves and
Rachael and Phillippa Corcutt

Once there was a white hare.
He lived on a little island.
The white hare loved the island,
but he was fed up with seeing
the same things every day.

2

3

Every day, the white hare looked
across the water.
He could see another island.
He wanted to go there.

4

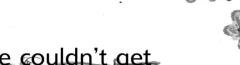

But the white hare couldn't get
to the island.
He couldn't swim.

He couldn't fly.

He didn't have a boat.
The white hare was sad.

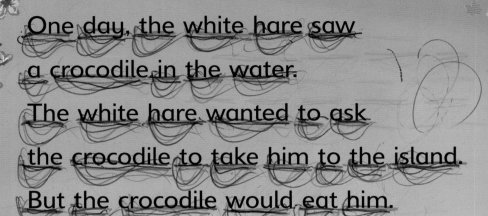

One day, the white hare saw
a crocodile in the water.
The white hare wanted to ask
the crocodile to take him to the island.
But the crocodile would eat him.
Then the white hare had a good idea.

"Hello, clever crocodile,"
said the white hare.
"May I ask you something?"

The crocodile smiled and swam closer.
"What do you want to know?"
he said.

"Crab thinks there are more hares in the world than crocodiles, but I think there are more crocodiles. What do you think?" asked the white hare.

"More crocodiles," said the crocodile. "We are more important than hares."

"Let's see," said the white hare.
"Go and get all the crocodiles.
Line them up, nose to tail,
across the water. We will see
if they go all the way to that island."

The crocodile went to get
lots of crocodiles.
He lined them up, nose to tail,
across the water.

They went all the way to the island.
"You see," said the crocodile.
"There are more crocodiles than hares."

"I need to make sure,"
said the white hare.
"Stay very still so I can count you."

The white hare ran across
the crocodiles, counting as he went.
"One ... two ... three ..." he counted.
The crocodiles stayed very still.

The white hare got to the island.
He had tricked the crocodile.
"Thank you for helping me!"
he laughed, and he ran off
as fast as he could.

18

Story order

Look at these 5 pictures and captions.
Put the pictures in the right order
to retell the story.

1

The white hare ran across the crocodiles.

2

The white hare was fed up.

3

The crocodile got lots of crocodiles.

4

The white hare laughed and ran away.

5

The crocodile said he was more important.

Guide for Independent Reading

This series is designed to provide an opportunity for your child to read on their own. These notes are written for you to help your child choose a book and to read it independently.

In school, your child's teacher will often be using reading books which have been banded to support the process of learning to read. Use the book band colour your child is reading in school to help you make a good choice. *The White Hare and the Crocodile* is a good choice for children reading at Turquoise Band in their classroom to read independently. The aim of independent reading is to read this book with ease, so that your child enjoys the story and relates it to their own experiences.

About the book

In this Japanese tale, a white hare is determined to see the world and tries to trick a crocodile into helping him.

Before reading

Help your child to learn how to make good choices by asking: "Why did you choose this book? Why do you think you will enjoy it?" Look at the cover together and ask: "What do you think the story will be about?" Ask your child to think of what they already know about the story context. Then ask your child to read the title aloud. Ask: "What do you think the white hare will be doing in the story?" Remind your child that they can sound out a word in syllable chunks if they get stuck.

Decide together whether your child will read the story independently or read it aloud to you.

During reading

Remind your child of what they know and what they can do independently. If reading aloud, support your child if they hesitate or ask for help by telling them the word. If reading to themselves, remind your child that they can come and ask for your help if stuck.

After reading

Support comprehension by asking your child to tell you about the story. Use the story order puzzle to encourage your child to retell the story in the right sequence, in their own words. The correct sequence can be found on the next page.

Help your child think about the messages in the book that go beyond the story and ask: "Do you think the white hare will ever want to go back to his island? Will he be able to trick the crocodile again?"

Give your child a chance to respond to the story: "Did you have a favourite part? What did you think would happen when the crocodiles lined up?"

Extending learning

Help your child understand the story structure by using the same sentence patterning and adding different elements. "Let's make up a new story about the white hare. Where else might he want to go? How might he manage to get there?"

In the classroom, your child's teacher may be teaching about recognising punctuation marks. Ask your child to identify some question marks in the story and then ask them to practise reading the whole sentences with appropriate expression.

Franklin Watts
First published in Great Britain in 2022
by Hodder & Stoughton

Copyright © Hodder & Stoughton Limited, 2022

Series Editors: Jackie Hamley and Melanie Palmer
Series Advisors and Development Editors: Dr Sue Bodman and Glen Franklin
Series Designers: Cathryn Gilbert and Peter Scoulding

A CIP catalogue record for this book is
available from the British Library.

ISBN 978 1 4451 8421 0 (hbk)
ISBN 978 1 4451 8422 7 (pbk)
ISBN 978 1 4451 8503 3 (library ebook)
ISBN 978 1 4451 8502 6 (ebook)

Printed in China

Franklin Watts
An imprint of
Hachette Children's Group
Part of Hodder & Stoughton
Carmelite House
50 Victoria Embankment
London EC4Y 0DZ

An Hachette UK Company
www.hachette.co.uk

www.reading-champion.co.uk

Answer to Story order: 2, 5, 3, 1, 4